This Old Man

illustrated by Claire Keay

Child's Play (International) Ltd
Ashworth Rd, Bridgemead, Swindon SN5 7YD, UK
Swindon   Auburn ME   Sydney
© 2018 Child's Play (International) Ltd   Printed in Heshan, China
ISBN 978-1-78628-176-0   HH131117NBH01181760
1 3 5 7 9 10 8 6 4 2
www.childs-play.com

This old man,
he played one,
he played
KNICK-KNACK
on my drum.

With a
**KNICK-KNACK
PADDY-WHACK,**
give a dog a bone,
this old man
came rolling home.

1+ 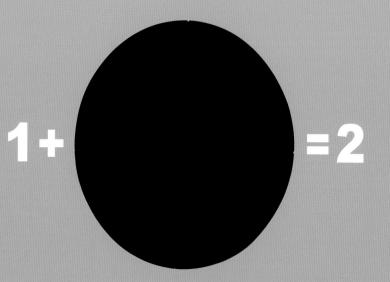 =2

This old man,
he played two,
he played
KNICK-KNACK
on my shoe.

With a
KNICK-KNACK
PADDY-WHACK,
give a dog a bone,
this old man
came rolling home.

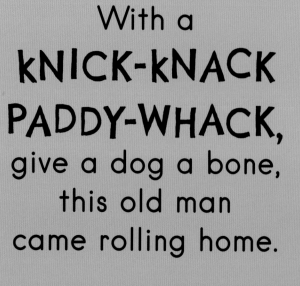

1+  +1 = 3

1+  = 3

This old man,
he played three,
he played
KNICK-KNACK
on my knee.

With a
KNICK-KNACK
PADDY-WHACK,
give a dog a bone,
this old man
came rolling home.

1 +  + 1 = 3

1 +  = 3

This old man,
he played three,
he played
KNICK-KNACK
on my knee.

With a
**KNICK-KNACK
PADDY-WHACK,**
give a dog a bone,
this old man
came rolling home.

1+  +2=4

2+  =4

This old man,
he played four,
he played
KNICK-KNACK
on my door.

1+ 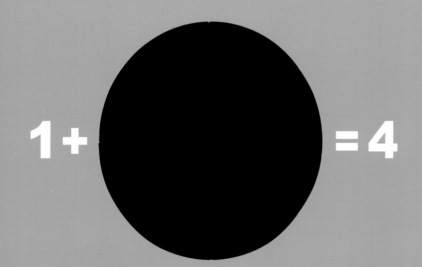 =4

With a
KNICK-KNACK
PADDY-WHACK,
give a dog a bone,
this old man
came rolling home.

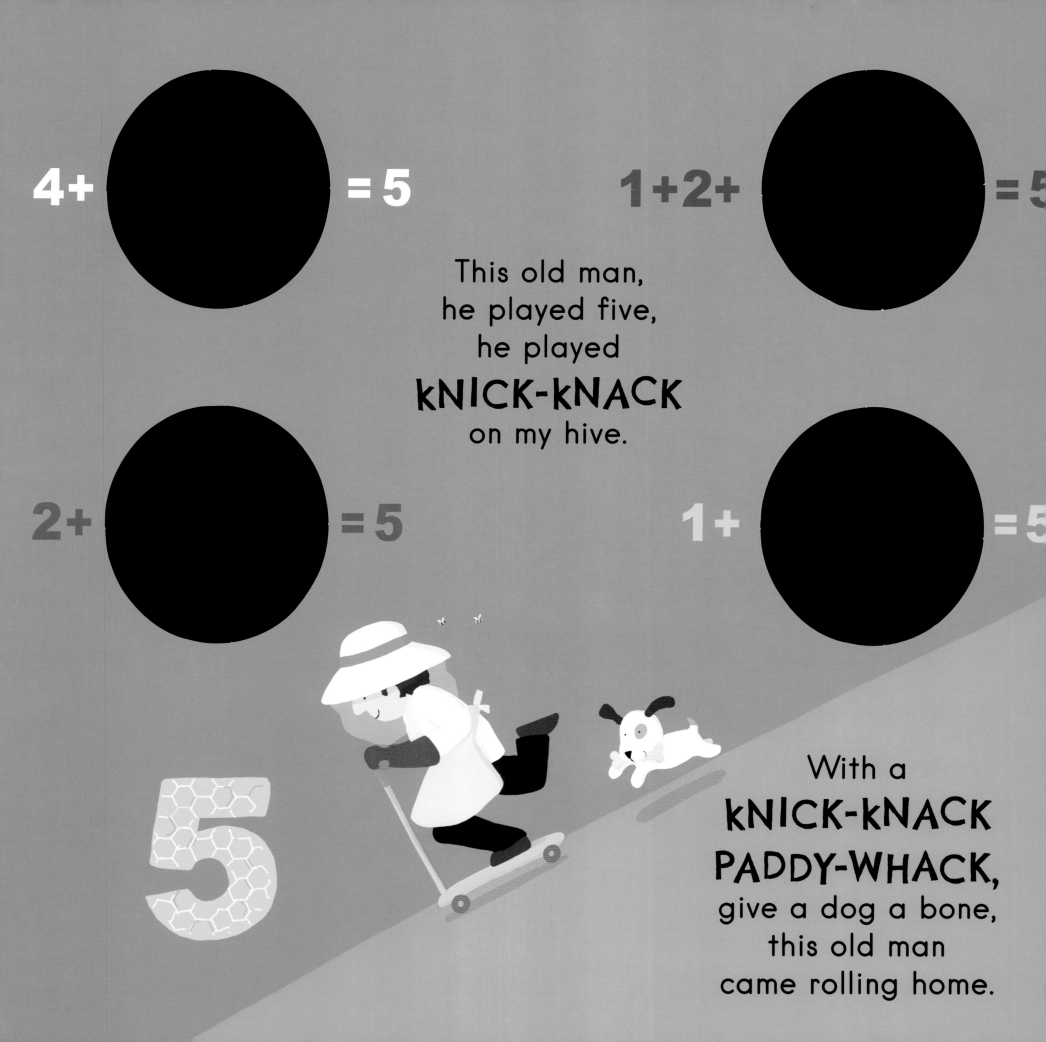

4+ ⬤ = 5

1+2+ ⬤ = 5

This old man,
he played five,
he played
kNICK-kNACK
on my hive.

2+ ⬤ = 5

1+ ⬤ = 5

With a
**kNICK-kNACK
PADDY-WHACK,**
give a dog a bone,
this old man
came rolling home.

5+ 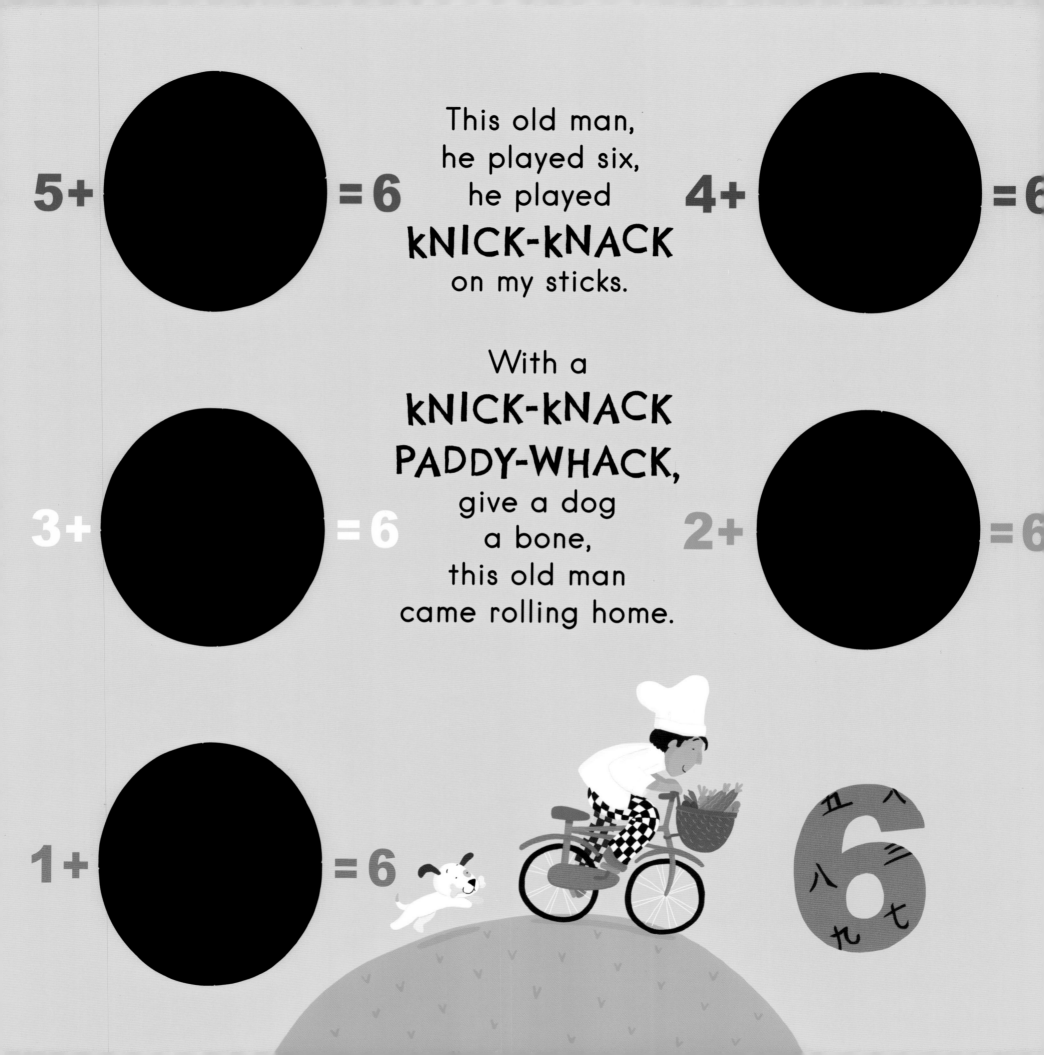 = 6

This old man,
he played six,
he played
KNICK-KNACK
on my sticks.

4+ = 6

With a
KNICK-KNACK
PADDY-WHACK,
give a dog
a bone,
this old man
came rolling home.

3+ = 6

2+ = 6

1+ = 6

6

$4 + 3 =$

This old man,
he played seven,
he played
kNICK-kNACK
up to heaven.

$6 + 2 =$ 8

This old man,
he played eight,
he played
kNICK-kNACK
on my gate.

5+4=  9

This old man,
he played nine,
he played
KNICK-KNACK
on my line.

9+1= 10

This old man,
he played ten,
he played
KNICK-KNACK
on my hen.

With a
KNICK-KNACK
PADDY-WHACK,
give a dog a bone,
this old man
came rolling home.